Rafu
AN AFRICAN JOURNEY

To Madison—

Joni Oeltjenbruns

Enjoy!
Joni Oeltjenbruns

Rafu, An African Journey

Based on the Ashanti parable,
"If you don't know where you've come from,
You won't know where you're going"

The Ashanti live in Southern Ghana, Africa. This culture is widely known for their mythology and folklore. Many stories told today are based on their folklore such as Anansi the spider and Brer Rabbit stories.

They believe animals have a spirit. The animals used in this story are the
- Sulcata turtle, known for wisdom
- Lion, known for mercy
- Monkey, known for creativity
- Vulture, known as Spirit God
- Porcupine, known as a lowly creature
- Dung beetle, known for transformation and renewal

Animal Trivia

Porcupines rattle their quills when they are frightened. They are nearsighted.

Dung Beetle also known also as scarab beetles, date back to the Prehistoric Age. They create their habitat in the dung of elephants, but long ago, created a habitat in dinosaur dung. They mate for life.

Dung Beetles were once a protected species in Africa.

Ashanti Words

Asante' (ah- sahn- tay') means *Thank you*

Jamba (johm'-bah) means *Hello*

The **Adinkra cloth** is pictured on the cover. It is a ceremonial burial cloth in the Ashanti culture. Each symbol stamped on the colored panels, signifies a character trait of the deceased person. The symbols are stamped on the weaved cloth with a calabash squash. You can find these symbols on the side of each page of the book helping you identify how Rafu is feeling.

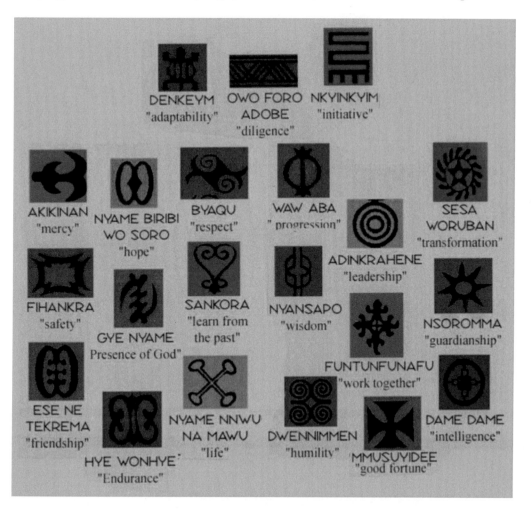

DENKEYM "adaptability"

OWO FORO ADOBE "diligence"

NKYINKYIM "initiative"

AKIKINAN "mercy"

NYAME BIRIBI WO SORO "hope"

BYAQU "respect"

WAW ABA " progression"

SESA WORUBAN "transformation"

ADINKRAHENE "leadership"

FIHANKRA "safety"

GYE NYAME Presence of God"

SANKORA "learn from the past"

NYANSAPO "wisdom"

NSOROMMA "guardianship"

FUNTUNFUNAFU "work together"

ESE NE TEKREMA "friendship"

HYE WONHYE' "Endurance"

NYAME NNWU NA MAWU "life"

DWENNIMMEN "humility"

MMUSUYIDEE "good fortune"

DAME DAME "intelligence"

DEDICATED TO ALL YOUNG LEADERS

A special thank you
to the students of the Owatonna High School Student Council
and their inspirational leader, Kory Kath.

Deep in the land of harsh
sun and shadows,
where the springboks prance,
thub, thub, thub,
the mangabey calls,
whup, whup, whup,
and the ibis flies,
flum, flum, flum,
lived Rafu.

Rafu lived alone in the shade
of a kapok tree.

In this same land,
Obadu emerged from his sandy burrow.
Rafu rattled and prattled his quills.
He hoped to scare Obadu away,
but Obadu was not bothered.
" I come everyday to sun on this rock," he said,
" I am too old and wise to be afraid of the
rattle and prattle of your quills."

Rafu remained hidden.
"I trod slowly and my eyes see only what is near," he said,
"I am a lowly creature with no meaning."
"There is meaning in every creature," said Obadu.
"My days of sun are few," he sighed,
"If you will bring me a
stone cup of water from the
Great Lake, I will teach you
how to find meaning."

Rafu brought a stone cup
of water. Obadu quenched his
thirst and paused.
"Meaning is found in life,"
his voice crackled,

4

"Journey to the Red Rock Valley. There, you will find
nine paw-sized stones. Bring them to this place
and lay them out in the shape of the moon's ninth day."

"But how can I complete such a task?" asked Rafu.
Obadu crawled to the edge of his burrow,
"If you don't know where you've come from,
you won't know where you're going. Your
journey must be completed in two days sun,"
said Obadu as he disappeared
beneath the sand.

Alone again, Rafu shuddered.
"Leave the kapok tree? But this is my home."
Obadu's words echoed in Rafu's head.
"If you don't know where you've come from,
you won't know where you're going."

Rafu sighed.
"Even a lowly porcupine must have meaning."
He waved goodbye to his beloved kapok tree
and began his journey to Red Rock Valley.

7

The path to Red Rock Valley was long and dusty.
The kapok tree was only a distant blur.

Rafu trod as the shadows stretched.
Rafu trod as the moon stole the sky from the sun.

8

The darkness was filled with strange noises
and Rafu's quills tingled. He longed for his home.
One day of sun had passed.

Stars illuminated the blue canopy over
Red Rock Valley, but Rafu struggled to see.
"Nine paw-sized stones," he repeated
as he scurried back and forth.

Two yellow eyes glowed from afar.
Rafu rattled and prattled his quills
as the shrewd eyes came near.
"What are you?" he cried.

"I am Lion,"
said the glowing eyes.
"Don't eat me!"
cried Rafu.
Lion's eyes glared,
"And why not?"

Rafu's throat felt tight and dry.
"Obadu sent me to gather nine paw-sized stones,
but my eyes strain to see in the darkness."
Lion's eyes softened.
"Obadu," he knowingly whispered as he
disappeared into the darkness.

When Lion returned, nine paw-sized stones
dropped from his mighty mouth.
"Asante', friend," called Rafu, but Lion was gone.

Rafu tried and tried to carry the nine stones, but his claws were too small. . . .

and his quills were too long.

14

Frustrated, Rafu plopped to the ground.

A nearby bush rustled.

Terrified, Rafu tried to rattle and prattle his quills,
but he was too tired to move.

15

"Jamba," said a voice in the twilight.
"Please don't eat me!"
gasped Rafu.

"Why would I eat you?"
said the voice.
"I am Monkey.
Who are you?"

16

"Hello, Monkey. I am Rafu. Obadu has sent me on a journey."
"My friend, Obadu," Monkey smiled,
"What kind of journey?"
"I must carry these stones back to the Great Lake,
but my claws are too small," explained Rafu.

Monkey bounded off and returned with
a woven pouch of leaves.
"This will help you complete your journey," said Monkey.
"Now, you must hurry," and he bounded away.
"Asante', friend," called Rafu, "Why must I hurry?"
But Monkey was gone.

Rafu place the stones into the pouch.
The morning sun warmed his quills heavy with dew,
but the dawn was soon interrupted.

A ferocious wind began to whip around Rafu.
Bits of sand pierced his eyes.
Twigs stabbed his tiny paws.
Harder and harder it blew.
"Where is the path?" cried Rafu.
The wind storm turned the light of day
into the black of night.

18

"I have failed. Two days of sun have passed and my journey is not complete." he wailed. The mighty storm raged all around poor Rafu.

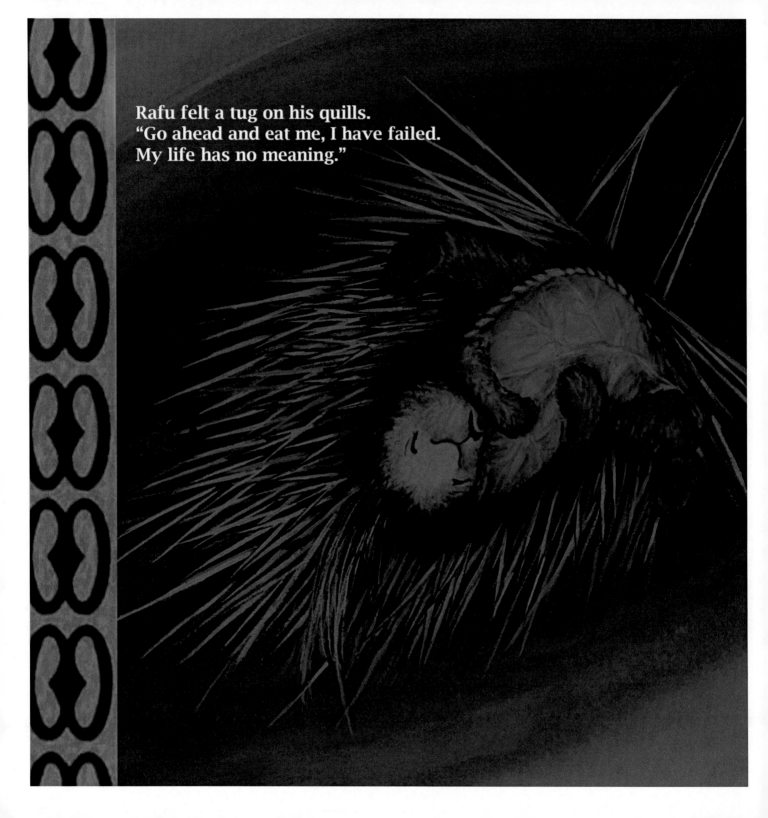

Rafu felt a tug on his quills.
"Go ahead and eat me, I have failed.
My life has no meaning."

Rafu felt another tug.
His quills scritched and scratched
as he was pulled across the rocks and sand.
His stomach churned as he spun.
Higher and Higher he twirled.
The wind's fury ripped at the pouch,
but Rafu clung tighter.

Suddenly, the winds ceased.
Rafu felt the warm morning sun.
Mighty Black Wings carried him
high above the swirling storm.

Rafu recognized the distant shores of the Great Lake. Closer and closer it came. His beloved kapok tree was in sight. Faster and faster the ground approached. Rafu closed his eyes as he plunged toward the ground.

23

Soo-ma-loom-loom!
Rafu toppled across the ground and landed
with a gentle thud. The familiar leaves of
the kapok tree waved in the soft breeze.
"I'm home," whispered Rafu.

"Asante', friend," called Rafu as the Mighty Wings disappeared over the horizon. The second day of sun had not yet passed. Rafu scrambled to arrange the nine paw-sized stones.

25

"Obadu?" called Rafu. Obadu was not in his sandy burrow.
"Obadu?" he cried, but Obadu did not answer,
only his mournful cry echoed across the barren land.
"I have completed my journey with the help of
Lion, Monkey and the Black Mighty Wings of the vulture,
but what have I done?" sighed Rafu.
"Where is the meaning in my life?"

26

Fleep. Fleep. Fleep.
Rafu gasped. He prepared to rattle
and prattle his quills, but hesitated.
"I am not afraid anymore," he said as he sat
on Obadu's large rock.

Fleep. Fleep. Fleep.
The noises came nearer.

Rafu turned to find nine baby tortoises resting on the nine
paw-sized stones. Their journey of life had just begun.
Rafu smiled. Now he understood Obadu's words.
"Meaning is found in the journey of life," he whispered,
"I can give to Obadu's children as he has given to me.
I can help just as Lion, Monkey and Vulture helped me.

The baby tortoise's eyes sparkled in the morning twilight.
"I know where I'm going," sighed Rafu, "My life has meaning."

And the springboks prance, thub, thub, thub,
the mangabey calls, whup, whup, whup,
and the ibis flies, flum, flum, flum.

Made in the USA
Middletown, DE
06 February 2015